Owen and Mzee

A Little Story About Big Love

Written + Illustrated by
Michelle Y. Glennon

Produced and published by GDG Publishing, LLC
Atlanta, GA
www.GDGPublishing.com

Copyright © 2007 by GDG Publishing, LLC

ISBN-13: 978-0-9787549-5-2
ISBN-10: 0-9787549-5-6

Library of Congress Cataloging-in-Publication Data available upon request.

FIRST EDITION: July 2007

GDG PUBLISHING, LLC™
ATLANTA
2006

Owen and Mzee

This is a little story about BIG LOVE. In a country called Kenya lived a 650 pound baby named Owen. He was a hippopotamus. He lived in paradise. There were beautiful mountains, very green palm trees and endless seashores. Birds of all kinds flew all around.

One day a little purple bird whispered in Owen's ear. "Will you play with me?" asked the little bird. Owen nodded, "Yes," with glee. They played "Hide and Seek" all the way to the top of a mountain.

Owen and the little bird climbed to the top of the mountain. They both looked down and in surprise saw a huge wave fast approaching their home. They watched the great wall of water come in and cover most of the land below the mountain.

After the wave was gone, Owen and the little bird started down the mountain. Owen asked the little bird, "Will you help me find my mommy?

"Yes, I will help you find your mommy and I will always stay and watch over you," promised the little bird.

Owen and the little bird looked
here and there and everywhere
asking, "Have you seen my mommy?"

When Owen and the little bird
arrived at Lafarge Park, they met Mzee,
an old tortoise, at the entrance to the zoo.
"Have you seen my mommy?" Owen asked.
"No, I haven't, but I would love to be your
mommy," Mzee said with glee.

8

This made Owen very happy.
The little bird chirped with joy, too.
Mzee added, "Owen, my baby,
you must know one thing. I am
a 130 year-old tortoise."
And Owen replied, "You make
a beautiful mommy."

From that day forward, Owen and Mzee became forever bonded as mother and son.

Mzee and Owen did everything together.

They ate together.

They swam together.

They sunbathed in the flowers together.

They played hide and seek together.

They took walks together.

They even slept together.

Then, one day, the park ranger noticed that Owen was acting more like a tortoise than a hippopotamus. He watched as Owen followed Mzee's every move.

13

The park ranger decided to introduce
Owen to Hildegarde, a 13-year-old
hippopotamus. Hildegarde had never
seen another hippopotamus and didn't
know how to act with Owen.

Owen decided to teach Hildegarde everything that he had learned from Mzee. How to eat, swim, sunbathe, play, walk and sleep — *like a tortoise*.

Today's Lesson:

How to be a hippo.

Eat

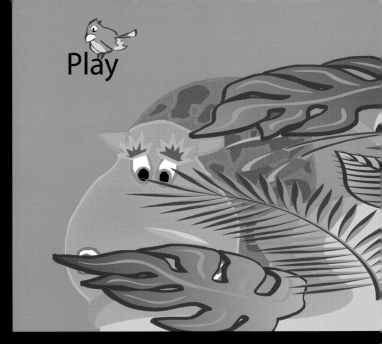

Play

Swim

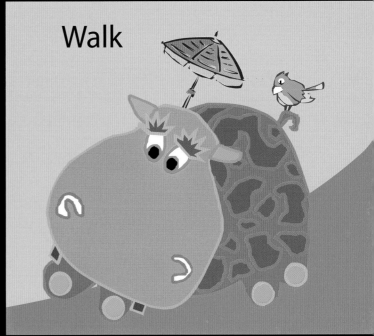

Walk

Sunbathe

Sleep

Owen liked his new friend very much but missed his mommy, Mzee. After a while, Owen became very sad. Until one day, the park ranger brought Mzee over to Owen. The two were happy again.

Owen asked the kind park ranger if Hildegarde could meet Mzee. The very next day, he brought Hildegarde over to where Owen and Mzee lived.

From that day on, Owen, Mzee and
Hildegarde always were together.
On moonlit nights, they liked to take
long walks together. They were all
very happy in their home at LaFarge Park.

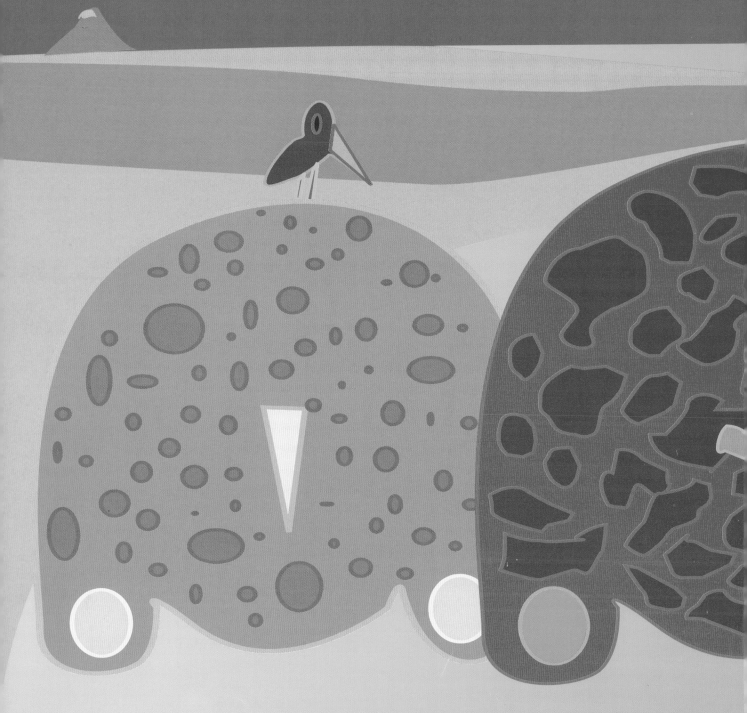

The story of Owen and Mzee is based on a true story. After the 2005 Tsunami, a baby hippopotamus named Owen was swept into the Indian Ocean. Wildlife rangers rescued him and brought him to the LaFarge Park in Mombasa, Kenya. There, Owen immediately adopted Mzee as his surrogate mother. Mzee, means "old man" in Swahili, is between 100 and 130 years old. It is true that Owen took on the behavior of an old tortoise.

AFRICA

★ Mombasa, Kenya

This book belongs to:

_____

My Name

_____

My Address

_____

My City and State

_____

My Age